Serena picked up on the first ring. "Hello!" she said, her voice bright and shiny.

"Hi, it's me. I can't believe I'm finally speaking to you. Your phone's been busy all afternoon."

"Oh, hi Chris." Her voice lost some of its glow.

"Were you talking to Drew all that time?" I asked.

"What if I was?"

"Well, gee, don't you two ever run out of things to talk about?" I said.

"You sound just like my mother, Chris. Cut it out, will you?"

"Okay." I shrugged, even if she couldn't see me. "I just wanted to tell you I'm sleeping in the barn now, so I won't be in the cabin if you try to call me."

"Why are you sleeping in the barn?" she asked, not sounding real interested.

"So I can be near Belle when her baby is born. Foals almost always come at night, you know."

"No, I didn't know. Listen, Chris, I've got to go. Drew may be trying to call me."

That hurt. Really hurt.

"He promised to call at seven and it's almost that now. I'll see you in the morning, okay?"

It wasn't okay. It wasn't okay at all. But what could I do? I hung up the phone. It had suddenly turned as heavy as wet cement.

So had my heart.

BELLE'S FOAL

The Double Diamond Dude Ranch
#8

By Louise Ladd

AERIE
BOOKS LTD.

This is a work of fiction. All the characters and events portrayed in this book are either products of the author's imagination or are used fictitiously.

THE DOUBLE DIAMOND DUDE RANCH #8: BELLE'S FOAL

Copyright © 1998 by Louise Ladd

Aerie Books Ltd.

First edition: December 1998

Printed in the United States of America

With love to Erika Louise McKeon and her first pony, Amber.

Acknowledgments

My deepest thanks to Jim and Bobbi Fetterer, Executive Directors of the Dude Ranchers' Association. They have willingly answered my many questions, come up with a number of wonderful ideas, and generously shared their knowledge of, and love for, dude ranching with me and you, the reader.

And a warm thank you also to Ellen Hargrave and Tony Bronson at the Hargrave Ranch in Montana, and the Foster family at Lost Valley Ranch in Colorado.

chapter one

"Crystal Bradley, what are you doing?" Maggie asked as I came into the barn.

"Belle's showing signs that her foal is going to be born any day now, so I'm moving in." I carried the folded camp cot down the aisle and began to set it up outside Belle's big roomy box stall.

Maggie lifted one eyebrow. "Does your father know about this?" As head wrangler, Maggie was in charge of all the horses at the Double Diamond, but my dad was foreman, so he was her boss.

"Yup," I said, trying to unfold one pair of the cot's legs. The hinge was rusty and stiff. "I told him my plan this morning and he agreed. Didn't he mention it to you?"

"I haven't seen him all day. He and Andy are out looking for the bull that broke out of the pasture. Here, let me help you." Maggie's long blond pony tail slid over her shoulder as she tugged on the other set of folded legs. She was tall, in her twenties, and was working to save up enough money to finish college.

"Chris, what do you mean you're moving in?" she asked. "Are you planning to sleep here every night?"

"Only until the foal is born." I felt something wet and warm nibbling on my ear. Belle had poked her head out the open top half of the stall door, curious to see what I was up to. "Cut that out, silly. It tickles." I shoved her head away.

"You know that mares like to be alone when they give birth, don't you?" Maggie asked.

"Sure, but I'm not going to bother her." I gave the cot legs a mighty jerk and they popped open. "I'm just going to be here to keep an eye on her, in case she needs help."

"Well, I guess if you want to . . ." She copied my jerk and her set of legs snapped into position.

We turned the cot upright and I said, "I'm going to the cabin for my sleeping bag and other stuff."

"Need any help?" she offered.

"Thanks, but I can manage. Be right back." I

gave Belle a pat and walked down the aisle, sniffing the fresh scent of the new wood that replaced the beams and stalls broken when the barn roof had fallen in at Christmas. We were fortunate that only the far end of the barn was damaged and most of the roof had held. I continued through the older part of the barn and stepped outside into the warm dusky air.

A Chinook wind had blown in yesterday and we were enjoying a mid-winter thaw. After the blizzard and the terrible cold weather that followed, it was great to be outside without your fingers and toes turning to ice.

Except for Belle, all the horses were out in the pasture, glad to be free under the blue sky that was now fading to dark. I wished my mare could join them, but Dad said it was best to keep her in the stall where she'd be having the foal so she'd be used to it when the time came.

When I reached the cabin Dad and I shared, I tried to call my best friend, Serena, again. The line was still busy. I wished the Changs would get call waiting, so I'd have a chance of getting through to her. I was sure she was talking to Drew Diamond again. The only thing to do was track him down at the ranch house and tell him to get off the phone so I could talk to her.

Drew and I grew up together on our dude ranch. His parents, Andy and Anna, own the Double Diamond and he was born only a year before me, so we'd been pals all our lives.

Until lately. Ever since Christmas, my two best friends—Drew and Serena—had been so busy with each other it was a wonder they found a minute to notice me. Serena still sat with me on the school bus while Drew rode in back with the other seventh grade boys, but that was about the only time we spent together. And her half of the conversation was usually filled with "Drew said . . ." or "Drew knows . . ." or "Drew thinks. . . ."

It could get real boring.

I checked through my duffel bag to make sure I had all the supplies I needed for the night. Granola bars, a big bottle of juice, flashlight, school books, a new horse story to read after I finished my homework. I thought about adding pajamas, but decided I'd better sleep in my clothes so I'd be ready if the foal began to arrive.

Zipping up the duffel bag, I slung it over one shoulder, my school bag over the other, and picked up my sleeping bag, pillow, and a couple of extra blankets. Loaded down, I made my way through the almost-dark to the barn. By the time I had my supplies arranged in the aisle outside Belle's stall, Anna was ringing the supper gong.

"Coming, Chris?" Maggie called from the cubbyhole office at the far end of the barn.

"In a sec!" I answered. I stepped into Belle's stall

4

and bent down to pet the stray orange cat I'd named Peaches. Her kittens were five weeks old now and cute as could be. Peaches had moved her family back into her chosen shadowy corner of Belle's stall the second the men had finished rebuilding it. She seemed to like Belle's company, and she tolerated mine by now. "I'll bring you lots of leftovers and more milk," I promised, picking up the empty dishes.

According to the rules, I wasn't supposed to be feeding her, since the job of a barn cat is to catch mice, but we had plenty of other cats to do the hunting so Andy pretended not to notice me sneaking food out to her. I'd caught him watching the kittens play one day, a big grin on his face, so I figured he was enjoying them as much as everyone else.

Maggie was waiting for me and we walked down to the ranch house together. "Heard from Jamie lately?" I asked her as we went inside. He was one of our wranglers who moved south for the winter, when we didn't have enough work to keep a full staff busy.

"I sure did. Got a letter from him this morning." She pulled it out of her pocket. "It's short, but he wrote it."

"That's great." I glanced at the neat printing. Lots of people don't like to write letters, but it would have been impossible for Jamie to write one six months ago, until we discovered his secret.

5

"He says, 'This ranch is okay, but I sure miss the Double Diamond,'" Maggie read. "'Tell Red Wing I vote her the best ranch cook in the business. Here in Arizona, the cook serves up rice and beans three times a day. We get other stuff too, but there's *always* rice and beans. I used to like them, but now I can't look at them.'"

She folded up the letter and put it back in her pocket.

"Red Wing will be pleased. I'll tell her." I took the cats' plates out to the kitchen and gave her the message.

"He always was a nice boy," Red Wing said. Her dark eyes and high cheekbones came from the half of her that was Cheyenne Indian. "Here, Chris, look what I got you on my trip into town today."

She opened a cupboard, took out a heavy grocery bag and handed it to me.

"Cat food!" I said when I saw the cans. "Does Andy know?"

"No, and he won't unless you tell him. That little Peaches is much too thin. She needs well-balanced meals while she's nursing those kittens. Leftovers won't do the right job."

"Thanks, Red Wing. I'll sneak this out to the barn right after supper." I hid the bag in the cupboard again and kissed her wrinkled cheek. She was one of my favorite people on the ranch.

The big dining room felt empty with only the few

of us gathered at one table. Dad and Andy weren't back yet, we had no guests staying with us during the dead of winter, and most of the staff, like Jamie, had moved to warmer places for the time being. In a way it was peaceful, but when you're used to big noisy groups, it was also a little lonely.

"Hi, Anna, how are you feeling?" Maggie asked as Anna dropped into her chair with a sigh.

"I'm okay, but I'm already as big as a barn and can't believe I still have almost four months to go." Anna Diamond glanced down at her round tummy. She was expecting twins in May, a fact that sometimes delighted her and sometimes scared her.

It was funny, but until Anna made the announcement, I hadn't noticed she looked plumper than usual. Maybe it was because she wore loose sweaters, or maybe because I hadn't been paying attention. Then suddenly, overnight, she seemed to get bigger, and bigger—and bigger.

Babies everywhere! Anna growing twins in the ranch house, kittens in the barn, and Belle about to have her foal.

What would Belle's baby look like? I wondered. Would it be a colt or a filly? Would she—or he— have Belle's pretty Arabian head and her smarts and speed? Or would he—or she—take after the wild mustang, Pirate, that Belle ran off with? He was a scrubby beast who'd wandered into the area a couple years ago and began stealing mares from all the ranches around. It's a stallion's nature to try to collect a harem, but the ranchers sure got tired of chasing after their best mares.

When we finally tracked Belle down in the mountains and got a glimpse of Pirate, we weren't much impressed. His palomino coat was scarred and rough, he had an ugly Roman nose, and he wasn't much more than sixteen hands high. Now Belle's just under sixteen hands herself, but so well-shaped—

"Chris, are you going to stir that chili or eat it?" Maggie asked with a grin.

"Oh! Sorry!" I'd been pushing my fork around the plate and didn't even know it. "I was thinking about the foal."

"Why am I *not* surprised?" she said. "Every other word out of your mouth for weeks has been about that foal."

"Let's change the subject then," Anna said. "How is school going?"

"It's . . . going." I couldn't think of a more boring subject to change to.

"Did you tell your mother about the C-minus you got on your math test, when she called last night?" Anna asked.

"Um . . . not exactly." I took a big bite of chili so my mouth would be too full to talk.

"In other words, no." Anna sighed. She was doing a lot of that lately. "Listen, Chris, school is important. How are you going to run your own ranch someday if you can't do the bookkeeping and keep up with the latest cost-saving methods? Ranching isn't just about riding horses, you know."

I nodded. Anna was in charge of running the business side of the Double Diamond, as well as taking care of the guests who came to stay with us. She knew better than anyone how much work it took, but I still hated being nagged about school.

Maggie seemed to understand. If Anna was like a second mother to me, Maggie was like a big sister. She said, "How is your mom? Did she meet with that record producer the Carsons introduced her to?"

"Yes!" I gave her a grateful grin. "He seemed real interested, she said, but he hasn't signed her to a contract yet."

Mom left the ranch, Dad, and me, when I was six to seek her career as a country western singer. So far she hadn't made it big, but I knew she would someday, and now it looked like it was getting close. All she needed was one hit on the charts and she'd be a star!

"Did she perform her new song for him?" Maggie asked. "The one she wrote when she stayed with us at Christmas?"

" 'One Guy, Two Gals' you mean," I said. "Yeah, she did, and he loved it, she said. He said it had 'real heart, real soul.' "

The "one guy" in the song was Dad, and the "two

gals" were Mom and Dad's lady friend, Amanda Morris. They were both here for Christmas and it made for a real interesting time.

Drew had been eating silently all this while, ignoring the rest of us. I figured he was thinking about Serena so I hurried through supper. My only hope of talking to her was to beat him to the phone.

Andy and Dad arrived just as I was finishing up my apple cobbler. They were cold and tired from their search.

"Did you find the bull?" Anna asked.

"At the bottom of a canyon," Andy said.

"Neck broken," Dad added.

Anna looked down at her plate. "That's too bad."

Ranching isn't an easy business.

While Dad and Andy dug into the stew, I slid out of the dining room and ran to the phone in the office.

Serena picked up on the first ring. "Hello!" she said, her voice bright and shiny.

"Hi, it's me. I can't believe I'm finally speaking to you. Your phone's been busy all afternoon."

"Oh, hi Chris." Her voice lost some of its glow.

"Were you talking to Drew all that time?" I asked.

"What if I was?"

"Well, gee, don't you two ever run out of things to talk about?" I said.

"You sound just like my mother, Chris. Cut it out, will you?"

"Okay." I shrugged, even if she couldn't see me. "I just wanted to tell you I'm sleeping in the barn now, so I won't be in the cabin if you try to call me."

"Why are you sleeping in the barn?" she asked, not sounding real interested.

"So I can be near Belle when her baby is born. Foals almost always come at night, you know."

"No, I didn't know. Listen, Chris, I've got to go. Drew may be trying to call me."

That hurt. Really hurt. But all I said was, "He was in the dining room two minutes ago."

"He promised to call at seven and it's almost that now. I'll see you in the morning, okay?"

It wasn't okay. It wasn't okay at all. But what could I do? I hung up the phone. It had suddenly turned as heavy as wet cement.

So had my heart.

chapter two

Belle's foal wasn't born that night, or the next, or the next. And I discovered that sleeping in the barn in the middle of winter wasn't exactly a cozy experience, especially after the warm Chinook blew away and the snow and cold rolled back in. I spent more time shivering than sleeping.

The barn would have been much warmer if there were more horses to help heat it up. I hear that in the East they keep most of their horses inside during the bad months, but our horses are used to staying out, unless a blizzard hits. The only ones sharing the barn with me now were Belle, Dad's favorite old mare Magnolia, and Drew's gelding,

Steamboat, who had a cast on his broken right foreleg.

Even if I slept in the barn, I could have spent the evenings in the warm cabin or the ranch house, but I was afraid Belle might have the foal during those very hours I was gone, so I bundled up against the cold and tried to do my homework wearing mittens. It wasn't easy.

"Hey Chris," Maggie called out one night as she let herself and a blast of icy wind into the barn. "Red Wing sent up a jug of hot apple cider for you."

"Thanks!" I closed my science book, took the thermos from her and poured a cup with shivery hands. "Umm, it smells good. Want some?"

"Sure." She sat down on one end of the cot. "How are you doing? Any signs of Belle going into labor yet?"

"Nope." I handed Maggie the thermos cup and found an almost-clean mug under the cot. I wiped it out with the edge of my pillowcase and poured cider for myself. "But I sure wish she'd hurry up."

"You know, I've heard that some mares will hold back and not deliver until they're left alone in the dark." Maggie took a sip of cider.

"But Belle and I are such good friends. She doesn't mind having me around." The cider tasted great, nice and spicy.

"This is her first foal," Maggie said. "It's hard to

guess how she feels about it. She may be nervous because she's never gone through this before."

My hands wrapped around the mug for its warmth, I stood up and leaned on the stall door. "Belle, are you nervous about having a baby? You shouldn't be, you know. It will be real quick and easy, I'm sure of it."

She stamped her feet and shook her head.

"Maybe she doesn't like being kept in the stall," I said to Maggie. "But we can't take a chance of her dropping the foal outside in this freezing weather."

"That's why your Dad is careful to breed the other mares so they'll have spring deliveries."

"I know. I sure wish I hadn't forgotten to bolt her stall door last winter. I knew she could lift the latch with her teeth. It's my fault she ran off and got pregnant too soon."

Maggie sniffed the warm aroma coming from her cup. "You're too hard on yourself, Chris. Look at it this way. All horses are counted as being one year old on January first. Since Belle's foal will be one of the earliest born this year, he'll be months older and bigger than the other yearlings. That might bring a better price when you sell him."

"Ummm . . ." I stared at the golden cider steaming in my mug. "I know I was talking about selling him, but maybe I'm changing my mind about it. I'm thinking maybe I'd like to keep him."

"Have you talked to your Dad about it?" Maggie

asked. "It's expensive to care for two horses, with the vet bills and the blacksmith bills and the vitamins and—"

"I know!" Since this foal wasn't part of the ranch's breeding program—thanks to that dumb wild mustang—I had to pay part of the costs of his care. "But maybe he'll turn out to be a fine colt—or filly—and Dad will think he's worth keeping."

"Maybe," she said, but she didn't sound real sure.

The kittens had been racing around in the straw, chasing each other and rolling around in play fights. Now the biggest, fattest one—the little girl with the tiger stripes—dashed for the stall door, made a flying leap and clung to the wood halfway up. I reached down and picked her up, snuggling her against my cheek. She batted at my straight brown hair, pretending it was some fierce beast.

Maggie smiled at the tiny thing. "Drew said Serena is planning to take the black kitten when he's old enough to leave his mother."

"She is?" I frowned. "She didn't tell me that."

Maggie didn't answer right away, then she said, "Chris, you haven't asked for my advice, but I know what's going on and I went through the very same thing when I was about your age. I know how you must be feeling."

"What do you mean?" I said, cautious. I don't believe in running around telling everyone my troubles, and I wasn't sure I wanted to discuss it with Maggie.

"When I was thirteen, my best friend began to date a boy. It was the first time either of us had a boyfriend, and she suddenly turned into a stranger almost overnight."

Wow, did that sound familiar.

"Carrie was so excited," Maggie went on, "so pleased that a real live boy was interested in her, she just about ignored me totally. I was so hurt, I cried myself to sleep every night."

At least I hadn't gone that far. Thinking about Belle and the foal kept my mind off Serena—most of the time.

"What happened?" I asked.

"After Carrie broke up with Ron, she was nice to me again. I never told her how much she hurt me, but when a guy named Peter began to pay attention to me, I ignored Carrie for quite a while. She found out how it was to be on the other side of the fence."

"That was smart," I said.

Maggie shook her head. "Not really. Being mean to her because she was mean to me was only revenge. What I wish I'd done instead was tell Carrie how I felt, really talked about it. She was a nice girl, and I think she would have listened."

"Didn't you tell her after it was all over?"

"No, we drifted apart. Hurting each other destroyed our friendship in the long run." She took a last sip of her cider and stood up. "It's even harder for you, Chris, since both Drew and Serena are your closest friends. I'd hate to see you lose either one."

Knowing she'd said enough, she handed me the thermos cup and strolled out of the barn.

I cuddled the kitten, thinking about her advice. Maybe I should talk to Serena—or Drew—or both—but how? What could I say? "Stop being mean to me?" That sounded so dumb.

But if I didn't say anything, would I lose Serena as a friend forever? And maybe Drew too? It could be awful lonely on our mountain ranch if I didn't have a single friend in the world.

I stayed awake a long time that night. I didn't finish my homework, and Belle didn't have her foal.

The next morning at the bus stop at the foot of the mountain, Serena and Drew, as usual, stood off to the side, talking. Their heads close together, they made a real contrast—blue eyed Drew and his reddish-brown wavy hair next to Serena's smooth black hair and dark, almond-shaped eyes.

I noticed I wasn't the only one bothered by it. The Hatcher twins, and Jimmy Thorne, who used to be Drew's closest friend, kept glancing at them too. Both Hatchers had taken to joking around with Serena, until Drew stepped into the picture.

Zeke and Josh looked so much alike—both beautiful blond hunks—that when they stood side by side you thought you were seeing double. When we were younger, I couldn't tell them apart until Josh scarred his chin coming off a bucking bronco. He was the wilder one, I came to learn, and Zeke was more of a clown.

"Hey, Chris," Zeke called. "Over here."

He and his brother had been making snowballs and they had an almost three-foot stack of them by now. Our parents were always afraid we'd miss the school bus, so they usually drove us down to the bus stop with plenty of time to spare.

I strolled over. "What are you going to do with those?"

Zeke grinned and pointed to Drew and Serena. "Give the lovebirds their own private snowstorm. Want to join in?"

"It won't work," I said. "They'll just get mad."

"So what?" Josh said. "Anything's better than watching those two fall all over each other."

To give them credit, Drew and Serena weren't as silly as some of the other kids who were "going together." A few couples in school acted like they were glued to each other, but my two best friends had the decency not to show off. It's just that they were always side by side, talking.

I glanced down the road and, way off in the distance, saw the bus coming. "You'd better wait till after school. If Mrs. Schultz catches you throwing snowballs, she'll make you sit in the baby seats for the next month."

The baby seats were for the little kids, up front, so Mrs. Schultz could keep an eye on them from her driver's seat. It wasn't much fun to sit with the giggling, sniffling, jabbering kindergartners during the long ride into town.

"I told you we waited too long." Josh poked his brother.

Zeke poked back. "Never mind. We'll get 'em good as soon as we get off the bus this afternoon." He turned to me. "So how's your mare doing? Any foal yet?"

"How did you know?" I was surprised. The Hatchers never talked about anything but football, basketball, and hockey.

"When we were over at your place helping you dig out on Christmas Eve, she only had a month to go. You made that fact known, loud and clear. So now it's been about a month, and being a math genius, I figured it out."

He'd noticed—and remembered! "Still no foal, but thanks for asking."

"I hear the sire is that wild mustang," Josh said.

He actually sounded interested in Belle! "Yeah, the one they call Pirate." I made a face.

"He stole one of our mares too," Josh said. "Right after he appeared in the area. She had a nice colt, ugly as a hog, but fast. Dad got a decent price for

20

him and the report is, he's showing signs of shaping up into a good cutting horse."

The bus pulled to a stop beside us. Mrs. Schultz eyed the pile of snowballs, glared at the twins, but didn't say anything as we climbed on board. She was almost six feet tall and ran her bus like an army sergeant. No one cared to mess with her.

"You've got good eyes, Bradley," Zeke said, following me down the aisle to my usual seat. "Thanks for spotting the bus in time."

"No problem." I dropped my book bag on the floor and took the window seat.

"Mind if I sit here?" Zeke asked, pointing to the empty space beside me.

"Serena usually—"

"Guess again." He jabbed a thumb at Serena and Drew. They'd boarded before us, still talking, and had taken the seat across the aisle. Together.

"Uh . . . then, uh . . . I guess you might as well," I managed to get out.

Zeke sat down beside me. Josh and Jimmy Thorne slid into the seat behind us! For years all the older guys sat together in the back and now, today, the entire bus was rearranged.

The fourth grade girls who usually sat behind me stopped for a second, surprised their place was taken, but after a few whispers and giggles, moved on to find another spot.

"I heard you talking about Pirate," Jimmy

21

Thorne said, leaning forward so I could hear him over the roar of the engine as the bus pulled away. "He made off with one of our good mares, too."

"Has she had the foal yet?" I asked.

"Um . . . yeah," Jimmy said. "But it had to be . . . put down."

"Why?" I gasped.

"It was born . . . all crooked. It couldn't even stand up."

"Oh no!" I said. "Why did you tell me!?" Panic stabbed me in the stomach.

"I'm sorry," Jimmy said. "I didn't mean to worry you. Dad said it probably wasn't the sire's fault. Sometimes that happens . . . you know it does."

You can't grow up on a ranch without learning that once in a while terrible things happen, but the idea of *Belle's* baby . . . I couldn't stand to think about it.

"Take it easy, Chris," Zeke said. "It was just bad luck. We bred one of our best mares to Jenkin's quarter horse—the stallion all the ranchers admire—and ended up with the worst colt in four counties. You just never can tell for sure what you're going to get."

"But I'll bet you'll end up with a fine foal, Chris," Josh said. "That's a real nice mare you've got. I saw you ride her in the dressage exhibition at the rodeo and I've never seen a horse with prettier moves."

It was good of them to try to make me feel better,

but I felt like a cloud of black smoke had fallen over me. I knew I wouldn't rest easy until Belle gave birth. And if she didn't hurry up and do it soon, I was going to turn into one huge quivering blob of worried jelly.

chapter three

. . . *Belle and I, racing across a meadow of wildflowers, the most beautiful foal ever born running at our side . . . He's perfect . . . so perfect . . . A man rides up to us, his saddlebags stuffed with a million dollars in cash . . . "No, thank you sir," I say, "I wouldn't take ten times as much for him . . ."*

"Chris Bradley!"

My head jerked up. "Homework" Brown stood over me, her arms folded. The entire class was watching, trying to hide their grins.

"I—I'm sorry. What was the question?" I asked.

"I asked if you were having a nice nap," Mrs. Brown said. "That was after I asked you the date on which General Lee surrendered near the end of the Civil War."

I blinked several times, trying to clear the blur from my eyes and the dream from my head. "Umm, I . . . ah . . ."

"Chris, please stay behind when the bell rings," Mrs. Brown said. "We need to have a little chat." She turned back to the class. "Now, who knows the date?"

Several hands went up but I didn't hear the answer. Gosh, it had been such a nice dream . . .

The final bell rang a short while later. Mrs. Brown asked Serena to tell the bus driver I'd be a few minutes late. Serena nodded. She'd been asked to carry the same message more than once this year.

"All right, Chris," "Homework" Brown said as soon as the room had emptied out. "What's the problem this time? You've been doing so much better since last fall, but recently you've begun to slide again. Not turning in your homework is bad enough, but to fall sound asleep in class isn't like you."

"I'm sorry," I said. "I didn't mean to . . . I just couldn't help it."

"Are you having problems at home, Chris?" She sounded like she really cared.

"No ma'am, I'm just waiting for Belle's foal to be born." I told her about staying near Belle, to be ready to help if needed.

Belle's Foal

"You're sleeping in a barn in the middle of winter?" Mrs. Brown said. "Is it heated?"

"No, ma'am, only by the horses, but I've got lots of blankets. Of course, I keep waking up to check on Belle . . ."

She gave me one of Those Looks, then shuffled through a pile of papers, pulling out the book report I'd turned in Tuesday morning. "I noticed a distinct change in your handwriting this week— that is, on the few assignments you actually completed. I barely managed to make this out."

I glanced at the scrawled words that wobbled all over the page. "It's hard to write neat when you're wearing mittens."

"Mittens?"

I explained while she shook her head as if she couldn't believe what she was hearing.

"Chris, I have to say, I've been teaching a great many years, and you are definitely one of the most . . . interesting students I've come across."

"Thank you, ma'am." I figured that had to be a compliment. I hoped.

"Now, you're telling me that this . . . crisis will be over soon, and you will return to your own bed once the foal is born. Is that correct?"

"Yes, ma'am. It could even be tonight. This morning I noticed Belle's udder has started waxing so—"

"Please, Chris." She held up a hand. "I don't need to know the, uh, specific details. I only want to be sure the situation—and your school work—will return to normal soon."

"Yes, ma'am, it will, I promise."

"All right, you may go now." Did I hear her whisper, *"Mittens!"*?

I glanced back when I closed the classroom door behind me. Her face was turned away but I saw her shoulders shaking. She couldn't be crying. But why would she be laughing?

Zeke had saved me a seat on the bus, and Josh and Jimmy were once more sitting behind us. Drew and Serena were together near the back, talking, talking, talking. What in the world did they find to say to each other?

Now that the twins were willing to discuss something besides football, basketball, and hockey, Josh asked me how living on a dude ranch was different from living on a regular ranch. I told them how I worked as a junior wrangler, taking guests out on trail rides during the summer, and about our pack trips and cookouts and all the other fun stuff we enjoyed so much. Then we went on to compare our different ranches—Jimmy Thorne's father ran sheep as well as cattle, for instance—and the trip passed quickly.

The twins' pile of snowballs was gone when we got to the bus stop. One glance told us what had happened. The parents waiting to pick up their kids were spattered with white!

"I don't believe it!" Zeke said, staring at his dad. Mr. Hatcher was knocking his hat against his leg, trying to shake loose a clump of snow. "They had a snowball fight!"

"With *our* ammunition!" Josh added as we rushed to the front of the bus.

Mrs. Chang brushed off her jacket and shouted, "Sorry, kids, I started it. I saw all those lovely snowballs, just begging to be thrown, so I thought I'd toss just one."

"Caught me smack on my chest," Mr. Hatcher said. "So naturally I lobbed one back at her . . ."

"Mom!" Jimmy Thorne stopped on the steps. "You're a mess!"

Mrs. Thorne pushed her sopping-wet hair away from her face and grinned. "I know. Who says only kids get to have fun?"

Zeke and I were the last ones out but we both had the same idea. Quick as a flash, we jumped down, scooped up snow, took aim and fired. Zeke's ball caught Drew on the leg, mine smashed into Serena's backside.

She squealed, grabbed up snow and got Jimmy Thorne on the neck. Drew's aim was way off, hitting Mrs. Chang on the arm.

In seconds snowballs flew thick and fast, grown-ups and kids packing and tossing as quick as we could, aiming at whatever target was handy.

The funniest sight was Mrs. Schultz' face as she

drove off in the bus. She couldn't believe the *parents* were breaking her rule about no fighting!

The fun lasted until we ran out of nearby snow and were white from head to foot. One by one, still laughing, we climbed into the cars and trucks and drove off in different directions, headed for our homes scattered around the mountains.

As Mrs. Chang drove the station wagon up our mountain, Serena chattered away, her cheeks glowing pink and her dark eyes flashing. At last the three of us were a group again—no, four, because Mrs. Chang was having as good a time as anyone.

"You got snow down my back, Chris!" Serena said.

"Well, you smooshed it down my front," I said, feeling the tickle as the cold stuff melted and ran down my chest.

"You *both* got me, back *and* front," Drew said.

"I'm soaked all over too," Mrs. Chang said. "Zelda Thorne has a good throwing arm, doesn't she?"

"So does Jimmy," Serena agreed. "But did you see me nail him? I knocked his hat right off!"

We went on talking and laughing all the way up to the Double Diamond. As usual, Mrs. Chang went into the house to talk to Anna for a few minutes before taking Serena back down to the Lazy B.

I saw my chance and grabbed it. It felt like the ice had finally melted between Serena and me—and Drew.

Belle's Foal

After Drew's puppy, Monster, gave us his tail-wagging, I'm-so-glad-you're-home greeting, we all headed to the kitchen for a snack, as usual, and found it empty. With so few people to cook for, Red Wing was taking the afternoons off. I'd spotted Joe Stillwater's pick up outside her cabin so I guessed they were on speaking terms today. Their relationship bobbed up and down like a raft on a white water river.

Red Wing had left a plate of fresh-baked chocolate chip cookies for us on the big square table and we divided them up, giving Monster his share, of course. He was the size of a half-grown bear by now, and still sprouting.

"Come on, Serena," Drew said, carrying his fistful of cookies. "I'll give you a chance to lose at Ping-Pong again."

"That's what you think." She started to follow him out the door.

"Hey, what about me?" I asked.

"I can't play against the two of you," Drew said. "It's tough enough to beat you in singles, Chris."

"Well, maybe we don't have to play Ping-Pong," I said. "Why don't we just . . . talk for a change?"

"Talk about what?" Serena asked.

"Just . . . *talk*. Like we used to do, the three of us."

Serena and Drew exchanged looks—and a secret message not meant to be shared with me.

"Hey, aren't you thirsty?" I asked, a little desperate. "Want some milk?" I grabbed three glasses out of the cupboard and opened the fridge door.

"Uh, yeah, okay." Drew came back to the table.

Maggie said I should tell them how I feel, I thought as I poured the milk. But how do I start? "I, uh, wondered if you'd like to come up to the barn with me, to check on Belle and Steamboat."

"I was planning to go up after Serena left," Drew said. "She can't stay long, so while she's here . . ."

"But maybe the foal was born while we were in school," I said.

"You know foals hardly ever come in the daytime." Drew drained his milk in one long gulp.

"But we could play with the kittens." I glanced at them over the rim of my glass. "The three of us."

Serena frowned. "What's wrong with you, Chris? Can't you see we'd rather . . ."

". . . be alone?" I finished for her. "Yeah, I sure can see it. I'm not blind, but *you* are."

"What do you mean?" she asked.

"How do you think I feel, being left out all the time?" I burst out. "You treat me like I've got some gross disease."

"It's nothing against you, Chris," Serena said. "It's just that Drew and I . . . want to be . . . together. Why can't you understand that?"

"I understand it, all right," I said. "But that doesn't mean I have to like it."

"You sure seemed to be enjoying yourself on the bus today," she said, grinning.

"What are you talking about?" I was truly puzzled.

"Zeke sat beside you going and coming. He's real interested in you, you know."

"No he's not!" I exploded.

"And so are Josh and Jimmy," she went on. "The three of them were hanging all over you today."

"That's crazy!" I said. "We just happened to be discussing Pirate at the bus stop, so we ended up sitting together. Besides, you and Drew started it, by going off on your own."

"Maybe we had a reason to," Drew said.

"What are you trying to say?" I demanded.

"We know Zeke likes you," Serena said. "So we thought we'd give him the chance to show it."

"Thanks for nothing!" I said. "I'm not interested in any boy, especially Zeke Hatcher, so you two can just mind your own business!" I slammed my glass down on the table.

Serena gave me a smile. "Liking a boy isn't as bad as you think, Chris. Why don't you try it?"

"And why don't you leave my life alone!" I stormed out the back door and headed for the barn.

Boy, those two had a lot of nerve, accusing Zeke of liking me! We were just friends. Anyone with brains could see that!

chapter four

More than anything, I wanted to saddle up Belle and gallop her high up into the mountains. I wanted to ride and ride and maybe never come back.

Of course I couldn't do it. Ever since Belle started showing signs that the foal was about to arrive, I hadn't even put the lightweight dressage saddle on her.

But I had to do something!

"Come on, Belle, let's get out of here for a while." I opened her stall door and led her out into the corral. There were only a couple inches of snow on the ground so I fetched the lunge line and fastened it to

Belle's halter. Maybe a bit of light exercise would make her feel more like giving birth.

At least it helped *me* to get out in the sun and fresh air where I could see the high blue sky and the mountain peaks that surround our valley.

"Okay, Belle, let's try a nice slow jog." I gave her the signal and stood in the middle of the corral, holding the lunge line while she moved in a circle around me.

"That's right, extend your stride like I taught you." She sure looked pretty, with her neck arched to carry her proud Arabian head and her tail held high as her long legs carried her over the ground, smooth as glass.

"Boy, those two sure are dumb, thinking Zeke might be interested in me. Have you ever heard anything so crazy?"

I clucked and Belle picked up the pace a bit.

The Changs' station wagon drove off and a few minutes later Drew headed up toward the corral. I concentrated on Belle, ignoring him.

"Hey, Chris." He leaned on the fence.

I turned my back to him. I wasn't interested in speaking to someone who'd said such stupid things only a short while ago.

"I just called Doctor Cooper. She says she'll take Steamboat's cast off in about ten days and X-ray the break."

I said nothing.

He waited a second, then went on. "That's the good news. At least we'll finally know . . ."

Something in his voice made me turn around. His face was kind of pinched.

I took pity on him. "Then what happens?"

"She'll put on another cast if he's doing okay. If not . . ."

We both knew that if the cannon bone didn't heal right, Drew would have to say good-bye to Steamboat forever. A horse is only as good as his legs, and on a working ranch there isn't room for an animal who doesn't earn his keep. It's just one of the hard facts of life.

"I'm sure he'll be fine," I said, knowing how scared Drew must be feeling.

"Yeah, Doctor Cooper said she thought so too . . ." He shrugged and walked into the barn.

A sudden gust of wind almost blew my hat off. I shivered and looked up. A heavy blanket of dark clouds had rolled across the sun that hung just above the distant western ridge.

"I hope that's not another storm coming in," I told Belle. "We've had more than our share already this winter."

The tiny figure of a rider appeared on top of the ridge, coming toward us. Belle made quite a few more circles around the corral before the rider was close enough that I could see it was Dad, riding Dandy hard.

I saw him check out the horses in the pasture as he passed by, then he galloped up to the corral.

"Have you seen Maggie?" he asked, pulling the palomino to a quick stop.

"She's not in the barn," I said. "She wasn't around at all when I got home from school."

"Take Dandy, will you?" He handed me the reins. "She was riding Cokey and he isn't in the pasture, but I'll check her cabin and the bunkhouse, just to be sure. Call the main house and ask Anna if she's down there."

"What's wrong?" I asked.

"She went out for a ride this morning, since it was such a nice day. Said she might head over to the wilderness area, but she should have been back at least a couple of hours ago."

"Were you out looking for her?"

"Yes, but I couldn't find her tracks. The wind is really blowing up there and it's probably snowing hard on the far side of the pass." We both looked out to the bank of clouds, quickly growing bigger and blacker. "When you talk to Anna, ask her if she's heard the weather forecast."

I tied up both horses and went into the barn office.

"No, she isn't down here," Anna reported when I told her about Maggie being missing. "I haven't seen her all day."

38

"Dad wanted to know if you've heard the weather report."

"I've been playing the classical station, but I'll tune in to the news and let you know."

By the time I had Belle rubbed down and settled snug in her stall, Anna called back.

"There's a storm coming for sure," she said. "Six to ten inches of snow expected, maybe more."

"I'll tell Dad." I saw him headed for the barn as I spoke. He's usually a real laid-back kind of person, but he sure was troubled now.

I gave him the bad news.

"We only have about an hour of daylight left." Dad spotted something behind me. "Here come Andy and Hank now. Chris, Dandy's had enough for today. Please bring Mouse, Lucky, and Samantha in from the pasture and start saddling them up."

"I'll come too," I said. "And Drew will help."

Dad shook his head. "I don't even want to think about you kids up in the mountains during a snowstorm. You'll save me a lot of worry by staying home."

I knew there was no arguing with him.

He mounted Dandy and rode down to meet the two huge Clydesdales pulling the sledge-load of hay up from the lower meadow.

I called Drew out of the barn and he gave me a hand bringing in the horses. Anna came up from the ranch house with thermoses of hot coffee, packets of sandwiches, and several warm blankets. She stayed to help us saddle up.

The men made search plans while they began to unharness the Clydesdales. As soon as the fresh horses were ready, their saddlebags stuffed with emergency supplies as well as the food, the three men mounted and rode off.

Drew, Anna, and I finished caring for the horses, then turned the Clydesdales and Dandy out to the snowy pasture.

"Maggie knows our land as well as anyone," I said as we stood watching the riders disappear over the top of the ridge. "I'll bet Cokey threw a shoe or something simple like that. She'd have to take it real slow coming back, but she wouldn't get lost."

"Then why didn't your dad find her when he first went up to look?" Drew said. "She'd stick to the main trail."

"Not if she was some distance from it and it was quicker to cut across country," Anna said. "Although there's a lot of deep snow up that high . . . but she's too smart to take chances."

"What about an avalanche?" Drew said.

We just looked at each other.

Anna shivered. "Come on, it's getting dark. Let's go back to the house."

* * *

Anna, Drew, and I had supper in the kitchen with Red Wing.

"That Joe Stillwater never could do anything right," Red Wing grumbled, dishing out the peas. "If he'd stayed another half hour, he'd have been here to help look for Maggie. Now he's back in town at his restaurant, instead of being useful."

"Are you blaming the man because he doesn't have ESP?" Anna said. "How could he have known he'd be needed here?"

Red Wing passed the platter of fried chicken to me. "He should have known, that's all."

I smiled in spite of my worry. Red Wing enjoyed complaining about Joe Stillwater almost as much as she enjoyed his company.

"Andy told me to call the neighbors for help if they're not back by nine o'clock," Anna said. "The Hatchers and Thornes know these mountains much better than Joe does, so give the poor man a break, Red Wing. OH!"

"What's the matter?" Drew asked.

Anna put her hand on her round tummy. "One of your brothers or sisters gave a healthy kick, that's all. Sometimes I feel like I'm carrying a football team in here."

"Maybe you are," Red Wing said. "You're already almost as big as you were just before Drew was born."

"Please, don't remind me," Anna said. "I don't want to think about it."

"What's that?" I jumped up and ran to the kitchen door. "I thought I heard a horse whinny."

I stepped out on the porch. Snow had begun to fall, the wind had died down, and the world was white, still and silent. I waited, but heard nothing more.

Going back inside, I shut the door behind me. "Maybe it was just one of the horses in the pasture."

We all looked out the window at the flakes drifting down, thinking of Maggie and the men looking for her on the mountain.

chapter five

It would be much easier if I was out there searching for Maggie, Belle." I paced up and down the barn aisle. "Waiting is the hardest chore in the world."

My book bag was on the cot, unopened. I was sure Mrs. Brown would agree that I couldn't think about math and history when my mind was filled with Maggie.

I glanced at my watch. Almost 8:30. In another half hour, Anna would call the neighbors and ask them to join in the search.

"It would help if I could talk to Serena, Belle. I

think I'll try again." I went into the office and punched in her number. Still busy.

"Darn that Drew!" I felt like I just had to speak to someone. Belle was a real good listener, but of course she wasn't much of a talker. I couldn't go down to the ranch house and leave her alone, but I wanted to hear someone say, "They'll find her. Maggie will be all right. Don't worry, Chris."

The wind howled around the barn. It had roared in from the west before we finished supper, whipping the snow against the windowpanes. We'd thought about bringing the horses in from the pasture, but the radio said it was a fast-moving storm that wouldn't hang around beyond morning. The few horses left out there would be fine in their lean-to's.

My hand was still on the phone. I punched Serena's number again. Busy-busy-busy.

I wished I could call Mom, but I knew she'd be performing at the club by now. She had a singing gig in Dallas this week.

Who else could I call? Who else would understand how I felt? Who else knew how rough life in the mountains could be?

Zeke and Josh knew. They'd been ranching all their lives, just as I had. I looked up the Hatchers' number in the address book. While I waited for someone to pick up, it came to me that if the Hatchers were needed to help hunt Maggie, it couldn't hurt to give them a little advance warning.

Either Zeke or Josh answered. I couldn't tell—they sounded alike on the phone. "Hi, it's Chris Bradley. Which one are you?"

"Oh, hi, Chris!" He sounded real surprised. "I'm Zeke. How're you doing?"

"Not so good. We have a big spot of trouble."

"Is it the foal?" he asked quickly.

"No, he's still not ready to get himself born yet." I went on to tell him about Maggie.

Then he said the words I needed to hear. "Don't worry, Chris, I'm sure they'll find her. Isn't she the tall lady with the blond ponytail?"

"That's her, all right."

"I remember talking to her when Joe Stillwater held his chili-cooking contest at your place. Hasn't she been at the Double Diamond forever?"

"Just about," I said. "She started as a stable girl when she was thirteen and has worked herself up to head wrangler. She's so good that Dad and Andy gave her the job over Hank, even though he's much older."

We went on to talk about what type of person makes the best head wrangler, then moved on to a foreman's duties, and somehow I found myself telling Zeke about Mom not liking ranch life. It was good to be thinking about something besides Maggie for a few minutes.

I was saying, "Mom wrote a song when she was here at Christmas that might turn into a real big hit—wait a second! I hear something!"

I dropped the phone, ran to the barn door and shoved it open. "Maggie!"

"That's me," she said with a tiny, tired smile.

She almost fell off Cokey when she tried to dismount. I caught her arm and helped ease her down to the ground.

"Where are the others?" I asked.

"What others?" She leaned on me as I led her into the barn.

"Dad and Andy and Hank!"

She dropped down onto a bale of hay. "I didn't see them. Cokey and I got lost."

I ran to get Cokey, pulled him into the barn, and closed the door. "I'll be right back!" I told Maggie.

I raced into the office and snatched up the phone. "Zeke! She's back! She found her way home! I've got to let Anna know!"

"That's great!" he said. "Tell me the whole story tomorrow morning at the bus stop."

"I sure will. Bye." I hung up and dialed the ranch house.

"Anna, Maggie just showed up! She's okay, I think, but she didn't see Dad or Andy or Hank. You'd better give them the signal to come home."

"Okay, but I'm not sure if they'll hear me over the noise of the storm. Are you sure Maggie's okay?"

"I think so, but she's real tired."

"Who wouldn't be? I'll send Red Wing up right away, and be there myself as soon as I signal."

I was kneeling in front of Maggie, trying to ease off one of her frozen gloves when I heard Anna's rifle. *Boom! Boom! Boom!* The signal sounded muffled by the howling wind and snow, but then maybe it was because I was inside the barn.

Red Wing arrived a minute later, carrying blankets and a thermos. "Maggie, you are a sight for sore eyes! Am I glad to see you!"

"And I'm so darn glad to be here. I wasn't sure I'd make it. Good old Cokey . . ." Maggie's voice trailed away and her eyes closed.

"You can't go to sleep yet," Red Wing said in her I'm-the-boss-so-listen-up way. "Can you feel your fingers and toes?" She knelt and began to slide Maggie's boots off.

"I don't know . . . maybe . . ." Maggie winced as one boot came off.

Red Wing pulled down her sock. "Your foot is bright red, but I don't see any white spots. You may not have frostbite—"

Boom! Boom! Boom! Anna fired the signal again. If she was repeating it, that meant she hadn't heard an answering signal from Andy.

"Here, drink this coffee." Red Wing poured some out of the thermos for Maggie. "We've got to get you

47

into a warm bath right away. Can you make it down to my cabin?"

"My cabin's closer," Maggie said.

"Chris, bring a couple of towels and those rubber boots from the equipment room. She's going to have to walk on her own. I don't think we can carry her."

"I'm okay," Maggie said. "I'll manage."

While Red Wing wrapped the towels around Maggie's feet and slid the big rubber boots on, I unsaddled Cokey and began to rub him down.

Boom! Boom! Boom!

We all stopped what we were doing and looked at each other. If Andy couldn't hear our signal, how could we tell him to come home? We knew the three men would stay out all night searching if they thought Maggie was still lost up in the mountains.

Anna and Drew showed up a couple of minutes later, each carrying a rifle.

Anna's face was stiff and pale. I noticed her coat didn't quite button over her big tummy. Drew was muffled up to his eyebrows in a heavy jacket and scarves and he wore a thick, knitted cap instead of his usual cowboy hat.

"Maggie, are you all right?" Anna asked, going to her.

"Yes, but I feel like such a fool, getting lost. I went much farther than I planned, so heading back, I thought I'd take a shortcut, but we were stopped by a huge snowslide and when we tried

48

make our way around it, the storm swept in and there was a sudden whiteout. I couldn't see a thing for over an hour but Cokey and I kept riding. We had to, to keep from freezing. When it cleared a bit, I didn't know where I was."

"You're not the first to get lost in a storm," Red Wing said, patting her shoulder. "Don't feel bad about it."

"But now three men are out there looking for me . . ." Maggie dropped her head.

"I have a plan. I don't like it," Anna announced, "but there's nothing else to do. Chris, will you go with Drew and ride to the ridge? The men ought to be able to hear your shots from there."

"Sure!" I said.

"I don't want to send Drew out on his own. It's safer if there are two of you to look out for each other."

"Let me go instead," Red Wing suggested.

"You haven't been on a horse in years," Anna said. We all knew she was thinking Red Wing was too old for a long ride in a storm, but of course none of us would say so.

"It's no problem, Red Wing," I said. "I want to go. It's not so awful far to the ridge, and if they can't hear us from there, we'll go on."

"*No!*" Anna's eyes looked like dark holes in the dim barn light. "The ridge and no farther. You have to promise me."

"But Mom—" Drew began.

"No buts! Do as I say or you won't go at all."

"Yes, ma'am," Drew said.

"We promise," I added.

She gave a sharp nod. "All right. Go get two horses from the pasture and start saddling up."

"Which ones?" Drew asked. "Jack went lame yesterday. We could take Magnolia." He pointed to Dad's favorite mare. He kept her in the barn at night because she was too old to stand the cold. "And Dandy should be rested up by now."

In the dead of winter, with no guests around, we only kept a few horses on the ranch, just enough for our own use.

"Not Dandy," Anna said. "He's not reliable under these conditions. Who else do we have?"

"What about the Clydesdales?" I suggested. "They're so big they'll push through the snow like it wasn't there."

"But they're draft horses," Maggie said. "They're not used to carrying riders."

"Um, well, actually . . . they are." I studied the toe of my boot. "I've been . . . riding them, now and then. With Belle pregnant, I thought it might be fun to try them out."

"Where did you find a saddle big enough to fit a Clydesdale?" Anna said, startled.

"I didn't. I rode them bareback, hanging onto a girth strap I rigged up." Without Drew, Serena or

50

Belle to keep me busy, I'd had to find *something* to do.

"Oh, for heaven's sakes." Anna was fed up. "That could have been dangerous. What if they'd thrown you off? When your father finds out . . ."

"It's getting late," I said. "We'd better get started, don't you think?"

"Crystal Bradley, you sure do try my patience at times." Anna rubbed her round tummy. "And to think I'll have two more to deal with soon . . ."

"Mom, don't you think we'd better get going?" Drew suggested.

She sighed and said, "All right, go fetch the Clydesdales."

Red Wing took Maggie to her cabin and Anna finished caring for Cokey while Drew and I brought in the gentle, giant horses from the pasture. Each one was almost twice the size of Belle, and looked even bigger in their shaggy winter coats. They were sweet, steady animals, and as strong as the Rocky Mountains.

Anna helped us rig up a girth strap for the second horse, then filled a couple of saddlebags with emergency supplies. We tied these and the rifles on with another strap in front of the saddle blankets she insisted we use.

Drew and I mounted with the help of a hay bale. It was a long way up to those broad backs.

We were ready to leave but Anna had last minute

instructions. "Fire the thirty-oh-six first, the one Drew's carrying. I'm sending the second rifle along in case the first one jams up, but you shouldn't need to use it."

"Yes, ma'am," Drew said.

"And Chris, stop at your cabin and put on extra layers of sweaters and long johns before you start out."

"Yes, ma'am," I said.

"You're headed due west, and the wind is out of the west, so as long as it's blowing into your face, you're headed in the right direction, but keep alert for landmarks, in case the wind shifts."

"We will," Drew promised.

"Now remember, go only as far as the ridge. The last thing we need is you two lost up in the mountains."

"Yes, ma'am," we both said.

She started down to the ranch house as we rode off, waving good-bye.

We followed orders and stopped at my cabin where I threw on extra clothes in record time.

Then at last we started for the ridge in the howling, swirling storm.

Two minutes later, I remembered.

"Drew!" I shouted. "I forgot about Belle! What if she has the foal while I'm gone?"

"Maybe she'll wait for you," he yelled back.

"I should have told Anna to stay with her!"

52

He didn't answer, only glanced my way for a second.

I knew what he was thinking. Ask poor pregnant Anna to spend a few hours in a cold barn, just in case Belle decided to have her baby? Even if I'd remembered in time, I knew what the answer would have been. Anna had enough problems without being asked to baby-sit my mare.

I'd have to trust Belle to wait for me. Right now, Drew and I had an important ride to make.

chapter six

Riding a Clydesdale is sort of like mounting an ocean liner after sailing a small boat. High above the ground, I clung to the girth strap and watched the horses' sturdy legs cover the ground at a rapid jog, their great heads nodding in time to the steady *cloppity-clop-clop-clop* of their huge hooves.

I was on Peanut and Drew rode Pansy. If we owned them, I would have named them something more dignified, like, maybe, Washington and Jefferson, but we only rented them from a Denver outfit for the winter, to pull the sleigh and hay-hauling sledge over deep snow.

"Can you see where we are?" Drew shouted over the roar of the wind.

"We just passed the middle pasture," I shouted back. "Remember what Anna said. As long as the wind is in our faces, we know we're going in the right direction, but keep a lookout for the windmill."

Guests who stay with us are often surprised to find we have windmills on the ranch. Most people think of them as belonging in Holland with the tulips, but here they do almost the same job, pumping water from wells to the stock tanks for our thirsty cattle.

They also make good landmarks to guide you through a storm.

The snow turned icy, stinging the skin around my eyes, the only part of me that wasn't wrapped up in layers of clothes and scarfs. I even wore two pairs of mittens, one inside the other. But I still shivered in the cold, cutting wind.

We jogged on and on, pushing through the drifts. After a while, the ground began to rise a bit and I knew we were beginning the long climb up the slope up to the ridge.

For a short time, the wind eased up some and Drew was able to talk without shouting so loud. "Chris, this horse is answering to my signals like a cow pony. Are you telling me you taught both of them to accept a rider in less than a month?"

"No, I didn't have to," I admitted. "They must have been ridden before. They were a bit skittish at first, but settled down right away, like they remembered a lesson they'd learned a while ago. Someone in the past did the work for me."

"Well, they sure do cover the ground, don't they?"

"Yup," I agreed. "It won't be long now."

The wind returned with extra force as we cleared the top of the ridge. We came to a halt. Drew untied the rifle and dismounted.

"Okay, here goes." He moved off a distance so he wouldn't spook the horses, aimed at the sky, and pulled the trigger.

Boom! Boom! Boom!

I sat silent on Peanut, shivering, waiting to hear an answer.

Nothing but the wind reached my ears.

"Try again, Drew."

He reloaded.

Boom! Boom! Boom!

Still no answer.

"One more time, Drew."

He slipped more rounds in the chamber.

Boom! Boom! Boom!

We waited and waited.

At last I said, "We'll have to go on."

"But Mom made us promise—"

"How can we leave our dads and Hank out here

all night? Just a bit farther and I'm sure they'll hear us."

He thought about it. "Okay, but only to the bottom of the pass."

He led Pansy to a boulder so he could mount and the big Clydesdales pushed on through the snow, down the steep slope on the western side of the ridge.

In front of us was the trail up to the high pass, deep in drifts. The mountain rising before us blocked some of the wind and it was a welcome relief. The cold gripped me hard, making my teeth chatter.

Drew slid off Pansy, walked a distance, and fired the rifle again. *Boom! Boom! Boom!*

Faint, but certain, we heard a soft *Pop! Pop! Pop!* to our left.

"Yes!" I shouted.

Then to our right we heard a slightly louder *Bang! Bang! Bang!*

"They must have split up to search different areas," I said.

"But they heard us! Now all we have to do is wait!"

"Turn on the flashlights so they can spot us." I switched mine on and Drew did the same as soon as he was back on Pansy.

A few minutes later, a shadowy figure rode out of the white darkness into the beam of my light.

"Dad!" Drew yelled. "Maggie's back! She found her way home!"

"That's great, but what are you kids doing out here?" Andy sounded gruff.

"Anna sent us," I said. "She tried to signal from the house but you couldn't hear her."

"She said she didn't want to send us, but it was the only way," Drew added.

Andy just nodded. He must have been a lot colder than we were, and darn tired too.

Hank found us a few minutes later.

"Where's Dad?" I asked him.

"I don't know," Hank said. "What are you kids doing way out here?"

Drew explained again, while I felt worry grow in me like a spreading sickness.

"Andy, Hank," I said. "Did both of you answer our signal?"

"Yup," Hank said. "It was real good news."

"But we only heard the two of you. Dad didn't fire back. Where is he?"

"He must still be on the far side of the pass," Andy said. He heaved a heavy sigh. "I'll go up there."

He was riding Mouse and the big gray's head was hanging low, his ears drooping.

"Our horses are fresher and stronger," I said. "Why don't Drew and I go?"

"Say, I didn't know those big Clydes could be ridden," Hank said, apparently just now noticing our horses.

"You kids are *not* going up the pass," Andy said. "I'll trade mounts with you, Chris, but first let's try to signal Bart again."

He fired his rifle and we waited.

The snow swirled around us as we sat silently shivering in the dark.

No answer.

Andy sighed again. "Okay, Chris, get down and take Mouse."

"Why don't I double up with Drew and give Mouse a rest?" I suggested. "Pansy can carry the two of us with no trouble."

"Good idea," Andy agreed as he climbed down. He's a big man and strong as a bull, but he staggered a bit as he walked over to us.

I pulled Peanut up beside Pansy and slid across, settling in front of Drew. He wrapped his arms around my waist and I snuggled as close as I could to him, glad to have my back protected from the wind. Hank boosted Andy onto Peanut and tied Mouse's reins to his own saddle.

"Okay, you three start back now. We'll catch up to you shortly," Andy called over his shoulder as he turned toward the trail.

"I'm not going back until I'm sure Dad's safe," I said.

Belle's Foal

"And I'm not leaving you out here alone, Dad," Drew said.

"Don't be so foolish," Andy said. "Get on back to the house. You're both half frozen."

"We'll wait," I said.

"Hank, take 'em home," Andy growled.

"Well now, Andy," Hank said in his slow way, "I'm not so sure that's a good idea. I'm not inclined to leave until we know you've found Bart."

"Are you disobeying my order?" Andy shouted.

"No sir, but I *am* questioning it," Hank said.

"Oh for Pete's sake! We're wasting time we don't have." Andy wheeled Peanut around and kicked her in the flanks. "Have it your own way, you stubborn fool!"

The huge Clydesdale broke into a gallop as Andy drove her through the deep drifts covering the steep trail. Up and up they plowed, disappearing from sight.

"Okay, kids, let's keep the horses moving so they don't freeze in their tracks," Hank said. "Did I ever tell you about the time I was caught in a blizzard during spring roundup out in Wyoming? This here is nothing but a little flurry compared to that storm. . . ."

Around and around we rode in a circle while Hank told us story after story of his life. He'd been a cowboy since he was fourteen, when he ran away from his home back East, so he had a good many

61

experiences to share. We'd heard most of them before but it didn't matter. A good tale-spinner like Hank can make it just as interesting the tenth time as the first.

At one point I thought I heard a single shot, but it was so faint I couldn't be sure. It could have been a tree branch breaking, or ice cracking somewhere.

I don't know how long we rode in circles and listened to Hank. Things like clocks and minutes and hours didn't seem to exist anymore. It was a world of cold, wind, snow, the warmth of Drew against my back, and Hank's stories floating through the thick air.

And then Pansy whinnied. We pointed the flashlights up the trail and here came Peanut down toward us. But it was just the one Clydesdale. There was no sign of Lucky, the horse Dad had been riding.

The beam of light picked up Andy, and in front of him, slung over the withers like a long sack of flour, was a man lying facedown.

Riding bareback, that's how you carry a man who is unconscious—or dead.

And the man was my dad.

chapter seven

I opened my mouth to scream but couldn't squeeze out a sound.

"It's okay, Chris," Andy shouted, riding up to us. "He's knocked out, but he'll be all right."

"What happened?" Hank asked for me.

"On the other side of the pass, the wind has blown big sections free of snow. His horse fell on an icy patch. Bart must have hit his head on a rock. It's only a small cut, and seems to be his only injury. I checked him all over and didn't feel any broken bones."

"How did you find him?" Hank said.

"His horse called to mine ... Lucky's leg ..."

Hank nodded. "I thought I heard a shot. Poor Lucky. He was a good one."

Andy glanced at Drew and me. "The leg was shattered. There was no way of saving him."

I swallowed hard, then sucked in a lungful of air. "Are you *sure* Dad's . . . okay?"

"Pretty sure." Andy nodded. "Come on. Let's get him home."

I don't remember the ride back. My mind was as numb as my fingers and toes.

I do recall bits of later on, like a series of slides flashed on a screen.

Anna and Red Wing, bent over Dad's bed with a needle and thread.

Drew, Andy, and Hank at our kitchenette table.

Towels, warmed in the oven, wrapped around Dad, yellow replacing green replacing pink as they cooled.

Red Wing helping me into a hot bath.

Anna on the phone with the doctor.

Clutching Dad's hand.

Feeling him squeeze back.

I didn't really come to until Dad did. I guess I just couldn't face the idea of life without him in it.

When he opened his eyes and looked into mine, I began to breathe again.

Sometime later, Anna came back into the bedroom. "The doctor says all the signs I reported look good and there's probably no need for you to make the long trip down the mountain, Bart. It might even make you worse."

"That's what I hoped to hear," Dad said. "I feel nice and comfy right where I am."

"He gave Red Wing a long list of instructions. She'll stay all night, and she'll have to keep waking you up every couple of hours to check for signs of concussion."

"I'll be fine," Dad said. "It's not the first time my thick skull has taken a pounding." He touched the bandage on the side of his head. "Who did the sewing?"

"Red Wing," Anna said. "She did a real neat job, too."

"It's easy when your patient is out cold," Red Wing said as she came in. "It's harder when they squirm around a lot." She gave me a glance.

She was referring to the time she put a couple of stitches in my knee. I was seven, and even though she froze the cut with ice and I couldn't feel much, I didn't care to be poked with a needle. She kept telling me she'd sewed up more cuts than most doctors and it wasn't worth the long trip into town for two tiny stitches but I guess I'd raised a fuss anyway.

"Chris, it's very late," Anna said. "You'd better go to bed, and plan to sleep in tomorrow. After what you and Drew went through this evening, I'll call the school and tell them you're staying home."

Any other time I would have jumped at the chance, but now I didn't like the idea. Since Dad was going to be all right, I realized I had a terrific story to tell. And since tomorrow was Friday, I wouldn't see anyone until Monday if I stayed home. A really great story ought to be told while it's fresh.

"Gosh, Anna, I don't mind going to school. I feel fine and there's an important science test I shouldn't miss."

She gave me a look. "Oh, really? Since when did you become so eager to take a test? Especially one that you've been too busy to study for?"

"I've been studying for it all week!" I said.

Well, it was *almost* the truth. At least I'd opened the science book every night. Maybe some of it had sunk in by staring at the pages.

"Anna," Dad said, "let her go to school if she wants to."

"But, Bart, it's after midnight."

"She can catch up on her sleep over the weekend." Dad closed his eyes. "Speaking of which, I'm going to take a nap until it's time for Red Wing to wake me."

"All right, good night, Bart." Anna went out.

"You're really, *really* all right, aren't you Dad?" I whispered.

"Honey, I'm an old rodeo rider." He opened his eyes and looked straight at me so I'd know he was being honest. "I've survived a lot worse than a bump on the head. I'm only sorry about Lucky. He was a good horse."

"Yeah, he was. Ranching is a hard life, isn't it?"

"That it is. But it's also the best life too. Right, cowgirl?"

"You bet!" I kissed him good night and went out, closing the door behind me.

Anna had sent Drew, Hank and Andy to their own beds long ago. Now she was buttoning up her coat—or trying to.

"I have an extra down jacket I could loan you, Anna." Red Wing sat in Dad's favorite chair. She was a handsome woman, but she did enjoy her own cooking so she wasn't a skinny person. Her jacket would get Anna through the winter at least.

"Thanks, I'll take you up on the offer," Anna said, wrapping a woolly scarf around her neck. "And thanks too for offering to stay with Bart. I'm so tired I'm ready to drop in my tracks."

"Growing babies is hard work and it's been a long night." Red Wing picked up her knitting. "Have a good sleep."

"I will. Chris, go to bed—and thanks for riding out with Drew to find the men." Anna opened the door and went out into the snowy dark.

I turned to Red Wing. "I'm wide awake. Maybe I'll make hot chocolate. Do you want some?"

"Sounds good," she said.

As I took the can out of the cabinet, I said, "I forgot to ask you—how's Maggie doing?"

"She's okay. I left her tucked up in bed with a couple of hot water bottles hours ago. There was no sign of frostbite so a good night's sleep should fix her up just fine." She yawned and dropped her knitting in her lap.

By the time the chocolate was ready, Red Wing was snoring away, nice and comfy in Dad's chair. I checked and saw she'd set the alarm clock to wake her in a couple of hours, so I covered her with a quilt and let her be.

I read a horse magazine while I drank my hot chocolate and was just draining the mug when I heard a soft knock on the door. Pulling my fuzzy blue bathrobe tighter around me, I opened it a crack.

"I saw your light on," Drew said. "I couldn't get to sleep, so I thought I'd stop by."

"Come on in," I whispered, pointing to Red Wing. He tiptoed over to the kitchenette table while I heated up more chocolate. "I stopped by the barn earlier, on my way up to the ranch house. You were so busy taking care of your Dad, I thought I'd check on Belle," he whispered.

"Belle!" I hissed. *"How could I forget her?* How is she doing?"

"She was a little restless, but maybe it was because of the kitten."

68

"What do you mean?"

He grinned. "I couldn't believe my eyes. That little girl tiger was sitting on Belle's back!"

"No way! How did she get up there?"

"My guess is she jumped down from the hayrack. That one's a real climber." He took the mug from me and stirred his spoon around it, trying to dunk the mini-marshmallows.

"And Belle let her stay?" I sipped my drink, trying to picture it.

"She didn't seem to mind. Her coat's thick enough from the winter weather that she probably can't feel those little baby claws. She was ambling around in her stall and the kitten was perched on her shoulder, purring away."

"I've got to see that," I whispered. "Let's go up to the barn right now."

He shook his head. "That was a while ago, so I doubt the kitten is still there, but maybe she'll try it again tomorrow. I want Serena to see it too. Maybe she'll change her mind and take the little tiger instead. That kitten is something else."

"Did you talk to Serena tonight?" I asked.

"It was too late by the time I got up to the house. I was afraid I'd wake up the whole family." He fished a mini-marshmallow out with his spoon and ate it. "You know, I was thinking, Chris . . ."

"That's a rare event," I said.

"No, seriously, while we were out there tonight,

doubled-up on Pansy, I was thinking how it was nice to have someone warm my front. . . ."

"And I liked someone protecting my back."

"And I was thinking about all the troubles, and all the good times, and you're always there to share them with. In a way, you're more of a sister to me than the babies Mom will have in the spring, if they turn out to be girls. I'll be so much older than them, but you and I . . . we grew up together. . . ."

He glanced up to where I stood at the stove and paused, but I just waited until he was ready to go on.

" . . . So maybe Serena and I haven't been fair, exactly. We can be together with you sometimes, as well as together alone sometimes . . . I mean . . . well, do you know what I mean?"

"Yup, I sure do." I felt a grin spreading across my face.

"So . . . well, that's all I came to say." He finished off his chocolate and stood up. "Guess I'd better get back to the house, before Mom discovers I'm gone."

Someone tapped a quick three raps on the door.

Drew and I looked at each other, surprised.

"Now who?" I went to the door.

Maggie stood on the porch, all bundled up against the storm.

"What are you doing here, Maggie?" I asked, still whispering. "Come in."

She glanced at Red Wing and kept her voice low.

"I woke up and couldn't get back to sleep. I had to make sure you found Andy and Bart and Hank, so I went up to the barn, thinking you'd be sleeping there again tonight."

"We found them all right, but it's a long story." I noticed she'd kept her jacket on.

"I want to hear all about it—later." Her eyes were bright and excited. "While I was in the barn, I took a look at Belle. I think this might be it, Chris! She's showing signs of going into labor!"

"Oh, wow!" I forgot to whisper and Red Wing jerked in her sleep. "Are you sure?"

"She's sweating a bit, and pawing the ground. She's real restless, so I'm pretty sure."

"That's so great!" I hugged her, then I hugged Drew. "The foal's coming at last!"

"Hurry up and get dressed," Maggie said.

"Oh! Right!" I was all set to run out into the snow in my pajamas and robe. "Be right back!"

No one ever threw on clothes faster than I did that night. I scribbled a note to Red Wing and Dad, then the three of us slipped out of the cabin and ran to the barn.

My feet barely touched the ground as I floated along on a big bubble of joy. Belle's foal was about to be born!

chapter eight

Belle was restless for sure. She kept shifting around in her stall, sometimes turning her head to peer at her heaving belly, as if wondering what it was doing to her. As Maggie said, she'd paw the ground from time to time, and her pretty reddish coat had a sweaty sheen.

We kept the barn lights dim and used our flashlights to check on her in the shadowy box stall.

"Mares like to be alone in the dark," Maggie had warned us before we entered the barn. "They can actually stop their labor if they find humans too bothersome. They'll wait until they have privacy, so let's not disturb Belle any more than necessary.

We're only here in case she needs help, and mares seldom do."

We sat on the cot that we'd pulled halfway down the barn aisle, so Belle wouldn't think we were hovering too close by. I'd stay put as long as I could stand it, then sneak down and shine the beam of light into the stall. I'd seen foals born before, of course, but now that my mare's time had come, I was as jumpy as a frog in a field full of flies.

"She's kicking her stomach with her back legs," I'd report to Maggie and Drew.

"She's lying down!" I'd report a little later.

"She's up on her feet again," I'd say.

This went on quite a while.

The mama cat, Peaches, had moved her kittens to the deepest corner of the stall and wouldn't let them go near Belle. Having given birth herself recently, maybe she understood how my mare was feeling.

"She's lying down again," I said. "Maybe this is it."

A few minutes later, she was up, peering once more at her stomach.

The next time I peeked, Belle was down again, and I saw something I found hard to believe.

Peaches crept out of her corner and went up to Belle's face, resting in the straw. Then she licked Belle on the jaw. Belle, instead of objecting, lay still, enjoying it. A few moments later, Peaches returned to her corner and Belle heaved herself to her feet again.

The three of us were perched on the cot, like crows on a telephone line, when the barn door opened.

"Dad!" I whispered, going to him. "What are you doing out of bed?"

He silently closed the door. "When Red Wing woke me up, she told me about your note. How could I go back to sleep when my daughter's mare is having her first foal?"

"Are you all right?" I asked. "Is it okay for you to be up and out?"

"I once rode a bull in the rodeo only an hour after busting two ribs coming off a bronco. Don't worry about me, Chris. How's Belle doing?"

I filled him in on her antics. When I told him about the cat giving her comfort, he didn't believe me.

"How could I make up something like that?" I asked, a little huffy.

"I guess you couldn't, but I've never seen anything like it," he said with a grin.

I looked down the aisle at her stall. "I've got to check her again."

"I'll come with you." Dad followed me, moving as soft as a deer.

"She's down again," I whispered.

"This might be it, Chris. I see the sac."

Belle's back legs were toward us and I saw the birth sac emerging. It looked like a glassy balloon, growing bigger and bigger. A minute later, Belle's stomach gave a heave and the sac burst, releasing the fluid. Belle swung around and sniffed it with great interest.

"This is her very first introduction to her foal," Dad said. "By smelling his fluid, she's beginning to get to know him."

I tore my eyes away long enough to signal Maggie and Drew. They quietly came down the aisle to join us.

"I see two feet!" I whispered.

"Good, they're the front feet," Dad said. "At least this fella isn't trying to come out backwards."

Each time Belle's stomach contracted, a few more inches of the legs emerged.

"There's his nose!"

With a couple more pushes, the entire head was born.

"Ooh, he's beautiful," I breathed. "Look, he has Belle's Arabian face."

"And he has a perfect white blaze down his nose," Maggie added.

The glistening wet neck followed. It was a miracle. Right before my eyes, an entire new life was entering the world.

"Here come the shoulders," Maggie said.

Once they were out, it only took a couple more

pushes and suddenly a brand-new baby horse was lying in the straw! I was filled with a sense of wonder and awe.

"It's a girl!" Drew said.

The tiny filly opened her eyes and tried to lift her head. Belle swung around and stared at her in surprise. Then she stretched out her neck and touched her daughter, nose to nose. She gave a soft nicker and—surprise!—the filly answered her!

"You don't hear that too often," Dad said.

"I knew she was going to be a real special foal," I said.

"She looks good, Chris, very good," Dad said. "Much better than I expected."

My chest swelled up, bursting with pride. "I knew Belle would grow a good one. What color do you think she is?"

"It's hard to tell in this light, but I'll bet once she's dried off, you'll find you own a palomino, Chris."

"A palomino! Next to a chestnut, they're the prettiest horses in the world!"

Belle and her baby lay in the straw, resting for a while, then Belle stood up. When she did, the umbilical cord that had fed the foal all these long eleven months broke. Now the foal was truly a separate little creature all her own.

"Oh how I want to pet her!" I actually ached with the wanting.

"Not yet, Chris," Dad said. "Give them time to get acquainted before we step in. They need time alone together."

Belle was licking her baby, starting at her tiny little mouth and nose, then working her way all down her coat.

"She's tasting and smelling her foal while she dries it," Dad said. "They're growing closer to each other by the minute. Sometimes humans step in to dry the foal, but that's a big mistake. It interferes with the natural bonding."

"Isn't it amazing that Belle knows exactly what to do?" I said.

Dad smiled. "Mother Nature *is* amazing."

The foal kept struggling to get up and Belle kept pushing her back down so she could do a complete job of it. But the filly was a determined little thing. Only fifteen minutes after she entered the world, she heaved herself up and stood gazing around on wobbly legs.

Her little mouth made sucking motions and it didn't take her long to find her mother's milk. I'd been handling Belle's udder often, so that when the baby first began to nurse she wouldn't be too ticklish. It seemed to have worked. Belle made no objection and the filly sucked away, her eyes closed with pure content.

Maggie brought the iodine solution and at last Dad and I entered the stall. While he took care of

protecting the cord from infection, I threw my arms around Belle, then, for the first time ever, I patted her little daughter.

"My dream came true," I said. "Belle, you've just given us *the most beautiful foal ever born.*"

The snow had stopped and dawn was lighting the sky by the time we left the barn. I was so happy I just about flew down to the ranch house.

Red Wing was in the kitchen, ready with hot coffee, eggs, bacon and pancakes. We fell on the food like a pack of starving wolves but I managed to tell her all about Belle's foal and how easy and natural and incredible the birth was.

"I can't wait to see her!" Red Wing said. "What are you going to name her?"

"I don't know yet." I stabbed my fork into a stack of pancakes dripping with melted butter and syrup. "It will take a lot of thinking to find the absolutely perfect name."

"How about 'Penny', since she's the color of a new penny?" Drew suggested.

"Too boring," I said.

" 'Goldenrod'?" Maggie suggested.

"Nope, it's not special enough."

" 'Honey'?" Red Wing said.

I shook my head.

"Take your time, Chris," Dad said. "You'll come up with the right name sooner or later."

Belle's Foal

Anna came into the kitchen, only half awake. "Why are you all up? I thought you'd still be in bed."

"Belle had her foal—and she's beautiful!" I started in on the tale again.

"I'll go take a peek at her, as soon as I've had a cup of coffee," Anna said. "And if you've been up all night, I'd better call the school and tell them you two won't be in today."

Drew and I traded looks. "We want to go," I said. "We have to tell everyone about the foal."

"You'll fall asleep in class," Anna warned.

"That's okay," I said. "Mrs. Brown is used to it by now."

That was a mistake. Anna and Dad pried the story out of me. I ended up promising I'd work extra hard to make up for the stuff I'd missed this week. I didn't mind. I like getting good grades. It was just that sometimes real life was a lot more interesting than schoolwork.

In the car on the way down to pick up Serena at the Lazy B, I caught Drew yawning a couple of times. I thought I was still bright and lively, but it's funny how yawns are catching. Soon we were taking turns, all the while trying to hide it from Anna so she wouldn't take us back to the Double Diamond and put us to bed.

We both perked up when we got to the Lazy B

and Serena came out the door. I rolled down my window, about to shout out the news but she beat me to it.

"Did you find them?" she called as she ran to the car.

"Find who?" I couldn't think for a minute.

"Your Dad, and Andy and Hank!" she said.

"Oh!" Belle's foal had knocked everything else from my mind.

"Yes, we found them," Drew said. "We took the Clydesdales and—"

"We'll tell you all about it," I interrupted. "But first—it happened! Belle had her foal last night!"

"No kidding!" she said, beaming.

"And guess what?" I grinned, because I knew she'd love it. "It's a palomino filly! And she's beautiful!"

"A *palomino*! Oh, Chris, you're so lucky! Tell me every single detail."

So I did, the rest of the way down the mountain. Drew added a comment here and there, but Serena paid much more attention to me. It was just like in the good old days.

At the bus stop, Zeke and Josh dashed over to our car the moment Anna stopped. "Did you find them?"

This time I knew what he was asking. "Yes, and Belle had her foal too!"

I started all over again, and it took the entire trip

to school to tell both stories right. Drew and Serena sat across the aisle from Zeke and me and the entire busfull of kids listened to every word.

You could say that Drew and I were the stars of the school that day. All the attention helped keep us awake too. I whizzed through the science test, and I think I maybe even passed it.

It wasn't until we got home that I realized I'd forgotten about a really big problem.

Naturally, Serena and Mrs. Chang came straight to the barn with us to see the foal. The filly was frisking around, but the moment she saw us, she ran to Belle and hid behind her big mama.

I went into the stall and began talking to her while I ran my hands over her tiny body. It's important that foals get used to being touched right from the beginning. You could say it's the very first step in training them.

Slowly I guided her out from behind her mother.

"Ooh, she's so *darling*!" Serena cooed.

"She's *adorable*," Mrs. Chang agreed.

"Look at these long legs," I said. "They look a little spindly right now, but you can tell she's going to be fast and strong. See how deep her chest is? And look at her hindquarters. See the long croup and short cannon?"

The word "cannon" did it. I looked up at Drew, who had gone pale. His horse, Steamboat, broke his cannon bone when the barn roof fell in.

And in little more than a week, the vet would X-ray the bone to see if it was healing right. If it was healing wrong . . .

I don't think Serena or her mother noticed my pause. They were too busy oohing and aahing over Belle's baby. A minute later, I saw Drew walk down the aisle to Steamboat's stall. He was still talking quietly to his horse when the rest of us finally left the barn.

I called Mom in Dallas right after the phone rates went down at five o'clock.

"Belle had her foal!" I went on to give her all the details. I'd told the story so often now, I was pretty good at it.

"That's terrific, Crystal!" she said. "She sounds just lovely! And guess what? I have good news too. I've just signed a contract to record my new song!"

"The one you wrote at Christmas?" I said, delighted.

"Yup, and the producer wants to hear the rest of the songs I wrote. This could be it! My big break!"

"Oh, Mom, that's so fantastic!" We talked about it for a while, then I told her about Maggie getting lost, and how we finally found Andy and Hank— and Dad.

"Is Bart okay?" she asked. "I mean, *really* okay?"

"Yup, he says he's been through a lot worse."

"I *know* he has," Mom said, a touch fierce. "I

84

nursed him through a broken collarbone, and two broken arms. Take my advice, Crystal, and never marry a cowboy if you want a husband who stays in one piece."

"I don't want a husband at all, thank you anyway." I was in our cabin and I'd built a fire to take some of the chill out of the room. Now I watched the flames dancing up the chimney. "But you know what, Mom? I was thinking a little while ago. I told you about how Drew and Serena were always going off by themselves, leaving me behind."

"Yes, I remember," Mom said.

"Well, I think we're going to be doing more things together now, the three of us. But last night, after Belle had her baby, Dad said we had to leave them alone together for a little while, so they could really get to know each other. Is that why Drew and Serena want to be alone together?"

"Why, I never thought of it that way, but I guess it is," Mom said. "I remember when I first met your daddy, he suddenly became the one and *only* person I cared about. All I could think of was him, and wanting to be with him, and wishing the rest of the world would go away and leave us alone."

"So I guess it's nature's way, and I shouldn't mind too much if Drew and Serena go off by themselves sometimes." I felt a weight lift off me, like a heavy coat that turned to mist and floated away. "It's easier to put up with a thing you don't like when you understand it."

"That's true," Mom said.

"Okay, but I'm glad *I* don't feel that way about any boy." I thought of Zeke for a second. Nope, he was turning out to be an interesting friend, but that's all he was. I'd found out he could talk about stuff besides football and hockey and basketball, but I sure didn't feel like spending all my time alone together with him.

"Maybe you'll feel it someday, honey," Mom said. "But you've got all the time in the world, so don't worry about it now."

We went back to talking about the filly and Mom's recording contract. When I hung up, I felt better. I usually do after talking to Mom.

Nine days later, Dr. Cooper came up to the ranch, took the cast off Steamboat's leg and X-rayed it. She held the film up to a light and studied it.

"What do you see?" Drew asked, his lips so tense he could hardly talk.

"I see a nice clean break that's healing up just the way it should." She grinned.

"Yipeee!" Drew whipped off his hat and tossed it in the air. Then he grabbed me and whirled me around and around.

"Hey, I'm getting dizzy," I finally said.

"Then I'll spin you the other way." And he did.

A little while later, I went outside the barn. A warm wind had blown in and we were enjoying another thaw.

The corral was bare of snow so, for the very first time in her life, the filly was outside in the sunshine with Belle, getting her first look at the huge sky and the Rocky Mountain peaks.

I watched the tiny palomino kicking up her heels. She'd dash across the corral, give a little buck, then wheel and run back to her mama, only to dart away again. Her coat shone like a gold coin and her blond mane and tail blew like miniature banners in the breeze.

Drew came out to join me. "Thought of a name for her yet?"

"Nope, not yet. But don't worry, I will, and when I do, it'll be the perfect name for the most beautiful filly ever born, my Belle's foal."